For More, Please Visit

HollySymons.com.au

Aurelya in Wonderrealm

A Realmsverse Prequel

By HOLLY SYMONS

Sponsored Content (Totally Real Ads)

TRY OUR NEW

PLOT GLUE™

For when your story makes no sense and you stopped caring two chapters ago.

WHIFFLES'
PLOT COUPON
EMPORIUM
Because you deserve one convenient
excuse per act.

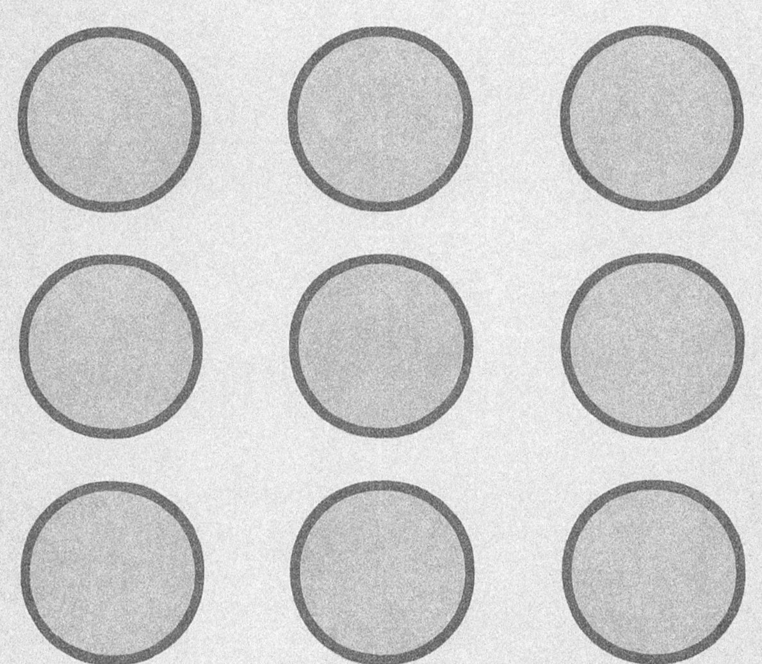

LOYALTY
PUNCH CARD
BUY 9 PLOT HOLES,
GET 1
DEUS EX MACHINA
FREE!

DISCLAIMER

Warning: May cause excessive meta-narration, spontaneous fourth-wall breakage, and an overwhelming urge to question the narrator's life choices.

Side effects may include:

- Talking to the author
- Talking *as* the author
- Losing the plot (*literally*)

Warning: May cause excesive meta-narratiation.

Spoiler Scrolls™
READ YOUR FATE EARLY!
Then ignore it and wing it anyway.
Now available in:
• Ancient Runes
• Cryptic Rhymes
• Passive-aggressive haikus

Aurelya in Wonderrealm

A Realmsverse Prequel

Table of Contents

Chapter 1: The Plunge into Pudding

Aurelya opened one eye.

Just one.

The world was... sticky.

And upside down.

Also, full of pudding.

Not metaphorical pudding. Not dream-symbolic pudding. Actual, honest-to-Realms, lukewarm pudding. She was face-first in it. Nose, eyelashes, and a good portion of her dignity, all submerged.

"Mmph," she mumbled eloquently.

Somewhere off to the left, a trumpet made entirely of toast gave a ceremonial *toot*. It was followed by polite applause from what appeared to be a pair of sentient oven mitts.

She pushed herself up dripping pudding and confusion and stared around.

The sky above her was lavender, streaked with polite polka dots. The trees were upside down, their roots in the air like awkward antlers, and their trunks dripping raspberry sauce. One tree winked at her. She pretended not to see.

"Ah! There you are!" called a voice that had no business being that cheerful this early in the nonsense. "You're late!"

A figure skidded into view on roller-skating carrots.

It was a rabbit. Or it used to be. Or it thought it was. It was, in fact, whiffles ears too long, bowtie too crooked, and wearing a waistcoat covered in tiny ticking clocks, most of which were labelled "Nope."

"You're late, you're late, you're wait, you're not even dressed! Where's your hat? Where's your invitation? Where's your fashionable sense of identity crisis?"

Aurelya blinked.

Whiffles didn't wait.

"You're wanted at the Feast," he declared, grabbing her pudding-covered sleeve and dragging her through what may or may not have been a hallucination made of jellyfish and abandoned homework.

"Feast?" she managed, still tasting caramel despair.

"Yes! The Realms Hatter's Feast!" Whiffles beamed. "You'll be fashionably early if we leave five minutes ago."

"I just woke up," she argued. "I think. Possibly. Maybe I'm still"

Whiffles shushed her with a spoon. A literal one. He pulled it from his coat and held it dramatically against her lips.

"Shhh. Don't say the word."

"What word?"

"Real." He shuddered. "Too triggering."

They walked (jogged? jelly-scooted?) past a talking bush that insulted her boots, a bench playing jazz, and a mirror that showed her as a sandwich.

Finally, she yanked herself free.
"Wait what is going on?!" she demanded. "Where am

I?!"

Whiffles gave her a sympathetic look, then reached into his vest and pulled out a scroll.

He handed it to her solemnly.

She unrolled it slowly.

WELCOME TO WONDERREALM
Your chaos has been scheduled. Please scream responsibly.
– Management

She stared.

Whiffles offered her a hat made of spaghetti.

"You'll need this," he said gently. "The scones are sentient."

Next, Time to meet the most aggressively ridiculous duo in Wonderrealm the jam-wielding, argument-prone oddballs: **Sir Crumbs and Spikeston the Impenetrable.** Get ready for sibling-level squabbles, teacake duels, and absolutely no clear plot advancement (on purpose).

Chapter 2: Sir Crumbs and Spikeston the Impenetrable

Aurelya's hat (spaghetti-based, still mildly al dente) had barely settled on her head before Whiffles flung her into a hedge.

"Just duck and roll!" he shouted.

"But wh…"

Thwack!

A jam tart whizzed past her ear like a sugary frisbee of doom. It splattered against a nearby tree, which promptly complained about stickiness and stormed off.

"INTRUDER!" someone bellowed.

Aurelya peeked over the hedge.

Two figures stood at the centre of what could only be described as a battlefield made of picnic rugs. They wore matching capes, mismatched socks, and far too much eyeliner for the time of day.

One held a golden teacup like a weapon. The other brandished a crumpet sword.

"I challenge thee to a duel!" shouted the taller one.

"I already won the duel, you crumb-coated windbag!" hissed the shorter one.

"Oh, I see them now," Whiffles whispered beside her. "The twin defenders of Confusing Side Plots: Sir Crumbs and Spikeston the Impenetrable."

"They look like they're about to hit each other with breakfast."

"They usually do."

Sir Crumbs turned, flinging jam into the air with a dramatic swirl.

"I, Sir Crumbs, shall defend the honor of this glade!"

"You spilled jelly in my sock drawer," Spikeston snapped, adjusting his armour made entirely of repurposed baking trays.

"You don't have a sock drawer."

"I DID BEFORE YOU ATE IT."

Aurelya climbed over the hedge and stepped onto the battlefield.

"Excuse me!"

"INTRUDER!" they both yelled again, this time in harmony.

Sir Crumbs raised his crumpet. "Declare your allegiance!"

"I don't know what's happening," Aurelya admitted.

"Suspicious," said Spikeston, narrowing his eyes.

"She's got pudding in her hair," Sir Crumbs noted. "That could be a sign of loyalty."

"Or betrayal," muttered Spikeston. "She smells of rogue tapioca."

"I don't know where I am," Aurelya tried again. "I was just told to come to a Feast... "
Sir Crumbs gasped. "THE FEAST?!"

Spikeston dropped his tray-sword. "She's one of the

chosen.”

“No, I’m just!”

Sir Crumbs fell to one knee. “Forgive our test of Valor, Noble One. You must be Aurelia.”

“Aurelya.”

“Right. Destiny mispronunciation is a common curse.”

Spikeston approached, squinting. “You sure she’s the one?”

Sir Crumbs sniffed dramatically. “The pudding never lies.”

Aurelya sighed. “Can someone please tell me what’s going on?”

Sir Crumbs turned to Spikeston. “Shall we?”

Spikeston nodded solemnly. Together, they chanted:
‘Wonderrealm is bending,
The Feast Day’s descending,
A girl with no clue
Must stumble on through,
To follow a plot

That we mostly forgot,
But it's fine
There's cake.'

Then they both exploded into confetti.

Aurelya stood alone, dripping pudding, holding a spaghetti hat, and now also covered in sprinkles.

Whiffles appeared behind her with a clipboard.

"You passed the duel test. Impressive."

"I didn't even do anything."

"Exactly," he grinned. "Classic protagonists move."

Next, prepare for the prickliest chapter yet, full of unsolicited wisdom, emotional metaphors, and the kind of cactus life advice that will stick with you longer than a glitter curse.

Chapter 3: The Talking Cactus Gives Life Advice (Unsolicited)

Aurelya trudged through a field of disappointed cupcakes.

They frowned up at her with judgmental frosting, muttering things like "Not good enough for ganache," and "Seen better sprinkles on a sock."

She ignored them.

Mostly.

Whiffles had vanished again (he did that a lot), and all she had to guide her now was the scroll in her pocket, which currently read:
"You are here."
Beneath it, a wobbly arrow pointed directly at her shoe.

"Helpful," she muttered.

That's when she saw him.

Or… it.
A cactus. Sitting on a velvet beanbag. Wearing glasses.

And sipping something pink through a curly straw.

The cactus turned slowly.

"Ah," it said, in a voice like aged philosophy and a mild sunburn. "The pudding girl arrives."

"I have a name," Aurelya said.

"Everyone does. Until they don't."
He sipped again. "I'm The Talking Cactus. Capital T. Capital C. You may sit, but I won't offer snacks. I'm still recovering from the Tapas Table incident."

"...Okay."

She sat on a small stool that immediately sank into the ground and vanished.

The cactus regarded her with the patience of a motivational speaker who'd been cancelled but refused to leave the stage.

"You are lost," he intoned.

"Yes."
"You are confused."

"Very."

"You smell vaguely of jam."

She sighed. "Is this more dream nonsense?"

"Ah," the cactus said, wagging one stubby spine. "Now that's the question. Is it a dream, or are you merely awake in the wrong genre?"

Aurelya blinked.

"What?"

"You've entered the Realm Between Stories," he explained. "A place built from half-formed plots, emotional metaphors, and budget hallucinations. Most don't survive without a narrator. Or a snack."

"Wait! so I'm... between stories?"

He nodded solemnly. "A girl caught between the tale she came from... and the one she's about to ruin."
"That's ominous."

"It's foreshadowing."

Aurelya folded her arms. "Okay, Cactus. Give me some

actual advice."

The cactus leaned forward.

"Fine. But you may not like it."

"I'm used to that."

He cleared his throat.

'Sometimes the path forward is full of sand.
Sometimes the people you meet are weeds.
Sometimes you bloom late.
Sometimes you're spiky.
That's okay. You're a cactus.'

There was a long silence.

"That's… your advice?"

"It's metaphorical. Deep. Resonant. Possibly
embroidered on a pillow."
"You're ridiculous."

"I'm emotionally drought resistant."

Aurelya stood up.

The cactus sniffed. "You'll miss me."

"I doubt it."

"You'll come back when you're emotionally dehydrated."

She walked away, muttering about talking plants.

Behind her, the cactus called after her:

"REMEMBER TO STAY HYDRATED - EMOTIONALLY AND LITERALLY!"

A moment later, a tiny bottle of glitter water fell from the sky and bonked her on the head.

Next, Let's plunge headfirst into the most chaotic garden party *never approved by a royal committee*:

Bring your mismatched teacups, dodgy rules, and emotionally erratic flamingos it's about to get bubbly.

Therapy Journal Page

"Sometimes the sharpest thoughts grow the softest flowers."

"Just because you're prickly doesn't mean you're not healing."

"Grow slow. Bloom anyway."

"Sometimes it's okay to wilt. Just don't forget your roots."

"Water your boundaries."

- The Talking Cactus

Chapter 4: The Garden Party of Chaos

The garden had opinions.

Big ones.

Aurelya stepped into the clearing and was immediately assaulted by colour and commentary. The daisies judged her fashion choices. The tulips whispered something about her "emotional posture." The roses just laughed.

A massive sign arched over the hedge:

WELCOME TO THE 4½TH ANNUAL REALMS HATTER'S FEAST
Attendance Mandatory. Sanity Optional.

A long banquet table zigzagged through the lawn like a drunk noodle. It was covered in mismatched teapots, glitter scones, sandwich towers, and at least three kinds of jelly that might have been sentient.

"Oh no," Aurelya muttered. "Not another Feast."

"Yes, yes, yes!" Whiffles reappeared, flinging confetti and breadsticks. "You made it just in time for

"

croquet!"

"I don't know how to play croquet."

"Good!" he beamed. "Neither does anyone else."

He shoved a flamingo into her hands.

It blinked.

She blinked back.

"Is… is this my mallet?"

"No, that's Steve. He's just helping today."

The ground trembled as a parade of Samurai Otters marched out of a flowerbed, each carrying a clipboard, a whistle, and an overwhelming sense of purpose. They blew their whistles and pointed to a field of bubbles.

"Your opponent is Gerald," Whiffles whispered, dramatically.

Aurelya turned.

A hedgehog in full chainmail waved at her.

“I can’t hit Gerald with a flamingo.”

“You won’t need to,” said Whiffles. “Just tap the right bubble before the music stops.”

“What music?”

BOOM.

A kazoo orchestra exploded to life from under the table, joined by maracas and someone sobbing into a triangle.

“Go!” yelled a penguin with a megaphone.

Aurelya leapt forward, Steve the Flamingo squawking as she swung at the nearest bubble.

It exploded in glitter.

The otters applauded.

A sandwich danced past her on tiny legs.

Aurelya missed the next bubble and stepped in trifle. Gerald rolled sideways, dramatically. A nearby otter awarded him extra points for flair.
“Is this scoring system real?” she asked.

"No," said Whiffles, sipping from a teapot filled with jam. "But it feels real, and that's what matters in dream-croquet."

Aurelya ducked, tapped another bubble, and Steve nipped her ear for unclear reasons.

"Do I win now?"

"No one wins," said an otter solemnly. "Only the garden does."

A cake exploded.

The kazoo orchestra reached a fever pitch.

Suddenly, the sky dimmed.

A hush fell over the garden.

The flamingo bowed.

Gerald saluted.

And then, music notes made of starlight rained from the sky, forming one sparkling word:

REALMVISION

Whiffles gasped.

Sir Sparkles rose from the mist, draped in a cape made of old receipts and sequins, whispering, "It's time…"

Aurelya stared up at the glowing letters and whispered back:

"…for what?"

"Rehearsals," said a voice behind her. "Darling, we need to rehearse the glitter cannon entrance."

She turned.

And saw him.

Next, Let's spin straight into the ultimate chaos sport where the rules are suspicious, the otters are overly intense, and the flamingos… may unionize.

REALMVISION

THE WILDLY NONSENSICAL TO DETERMINE THE GREATEST SINGER IN THE VAST MULTIVERSE

RULES:

- HATEFUL GLARES ONLY
- NO PREVIOUS TALENT ALLOWED
- SONG CHOICES MUST DEFY LOGIC

CONTESTANTS

Sir Sparkles Roarworthy

Drag Lion

SIR WHIFFLES RABBIT
Philosophher

SENTIEN KAZOO

SIR WHIFFLES
Rabit Phososer

BANSHE ON STILT

Welcome to Realmvision!

The Only Inter-Realm Song Contest That Requires Absolutely Zero Talent but Maximum Chaos™

Chaotic Rules

1. Bribing the judges is encouraged. The judges are bribable plants.

2. No autotune, but magical distortion is permitted.

3. If your act causes a minor reality tear, 5 bonus points.

4. Audience booing earns crowd-favor points.

5. Contestants may not transform judges into frogs. (Again.)

Contestant Bios

• Sir Sparkles Roarworthy – A lion-dragon hybrid who breathes glitter and sings power ballads in F sharp.

• Loki's Chaos Squirrel – Solo act. Backup dancers are invisible.

• The Shakespearean Penguins – Interpretive waddling meets iambic pentameter.

• Samurai Otters – Water drum acrobats with a vengeance.

• Madame Nutmancy – Predicts her own lyrics moments before singing them.

• Gary the Pigeon – Voted 'Most Likely to Poop Mid-Note.'

Chapter 5: Croquet with Samurai Otters

"Welcome to The Arena of Lightly Structured Mayhem," said an otter with a topknot and a clipboard.

Aurelya blinked.

The garden had transformed. The tables were gone. The cupcakes had retreated to the shrubbery (still muttering about her poor frosting vibes), and in their place was a croquet field... if you could call it that.

It looked more like a trampoline park designed by a confused jellybean.

The grass shimmered with stars. Bubbles hovered midair. There were wickets, but they were floating, spinning, and some were whispering threats. One licked its own post.

Aurelya held Steve the Flamingo tightly.

"Be brave," he squawked, "but not too brave."

Whiffles handed her a rulebook the size of a small pony.

"Here's the manual," he chirped.

"I'm not reading this."

"Good," Whiffles said, tossing it into the sky. It exploded into glitter. "Nobody ever does."

A line of Samurai Otters stood at the far end of the field. They wore ceremonial armour made of garden hose and spatulas. Their expressions were grim.

Sir Sparkles floated into the arena on a cupcake-shaped hoverchair.

"Contestants!" he announced, in a voice that sparkled with its own echo. "Today you play not for points, not for glory, but for something far more precious..."

Everyone leaned forward.

"...style."

Aurelya groaned.

A whistle blew. Gerald the Hedgehog rolled onto the field in a spiral of spikes and glitter. The scoreboard lit up:
AURELYA vs. GERALD

Game: Bubble-Croquet With Intermittent Interpretive
Dance Rounds

"Begin!" screamed a penguin referee, launching
himself into a somersault.

ROUND ONE

Aurelya swung at a bubble.

It dodged.

She swung again.

It turned into two smaller bubbles, both of which
insulted her shoes and popped themselves.

Sir Sparkles held up a scorecard: "7.2 for effort, -3 for
fashion."

The otters took notes.

ROUND TWO

Gerald launched into a dramatic roll, knocking over a
spinning wicket while also catching a butterfly midair.

The crowd gasped.

Aurelya tried to clap and accidentally elbowed Steve.

Steve bit her.

"That's a foul," muttered an otter.

"You're a foul," muttered Steve.

INTERMISSION: INTERPRETIVE DANCE ROUND

Sir Sparkles cleared his throat. "Each contestant must now interpret the concept of emotional bewilderment through dance."

Gerald did three perfect pirouettes and then wept into a leaf.

Aurelya stood still for a full thirty seconds, stared into the middle distance, and whispered, "I don't even know if I'm real."

The crowd burst into applause.
FINAL ROUND

Aurelya aimed.

The last bubble hovered, vibrating with destiny.

She swung.

Steve screamed.

The bubble popped.

A portal opened.

Everything froze.

The music stopped.

The wind held its breath.

Aurelya floated for a moment suspended in time before landing gently on her feet.

Sir Sparkles dabbed his glittery eyes. "That... was croquet."

Gerald saluted with a dandelion.

The otters clapped once, then bowed.

The scoreboard exploded.

In its place, a single spotlight beamed down on
Aurelya.

Sir Sparkles drifted toward her, microphone in hand.

"Congratulations, dear girl. You've made it to
Realmvision Rehearsals. And the theme this year is…"

He leaned close, eyes gleaming.

"…Unravelling in Style."

Realmsverse Croquet Rulebook

A bonus printable guide to the most chaotic, occasionally comprehendible game in all the Realms. This version is adapted from the Realmvision Festival edition. Play at your own risk.

1. Equipment May Move (or disappear)

Croquet balls may develop legs. Mallets may gain sentience. Don't ask questions.

2. Wickets Are Optional

Sometimes they shift. Sometimes they're portals. Sometimes they're made of jelly. Proceed anyway.

3. The Lawn Is Alive

Be mindful. The grass bites. Or purrs. Or sings depending on mood.

4. Points Are Awarded for Style

Backflips, puns, or causing mild magical mayhem will earn bonus points.

5. Disputes Go to the Goblin Referee

His name is Chad. He's emotionally chaotic but generally fair.

6. Winning is Subjective

You may win by reaching the last hoop. Or baking cookies for everyone. Depends on the day.

7. Audience May Intervene

Spectators may offer advice, chaos spells, or turn into ducks. Accept all outcomes.

8. Final Rule

If a unicorn sneezes, the game resets. Sorry.

Chapter 6: Whiffles Explains Absolutely Nothing

Aurelya was still glowing.

Not metaphorically literally.

Her hair sparkled. Her shoelaces hummed. Steve the Flamingo was now wearing sunglasses for his own safety.

"Why am I glowing?" she asked.

"You're finally metabolizing destiny," said Whiffles, who was busy making origami from a map that may or may not have contained spoilers.

They were sitting at a mushroom-shaped bus stop labeled:

TRANSPORT TO: UNFINISHED PLOT THREADS.
(Buses run every never.)

"I just won a bubble croquet tournament against a hedgehog in armor and now I'm invited to Realmvision," Aurelya said. "I'd like to know why."

"Because" said Whiffles seriously, "you blinked at the

right moment."

"That's not an answer."

"It's not the answer you wanted," he corrected. "It's the answer the Realm provided."

"Is there a plot?"

"Yes."

"Are we following it?"

"Sometimes sideways."

Aurelya groaned. "I need a map."

Whiffles brightened. "I HAVE FOUR!"

He pulled out four scrolls. They each unfurled dramatically.
   • One showed her face in the center of a maze labeled "Emotional Growth, Maybe."
   • One was just a large arrow pointing at a muffin.
   • One was upside down and on fire.
   • One said: YOU ARE HERE. But the "here" kept moving.

"I don't want a metaphorical map," she said.

"Then you're not going to enjoy the next scene."

A penguin zipped past on rollerblades holding a sign that read:

FORESHADOWING!

"Okay," Aurelya snapped, snatching the sign. "Real question: What is Realmvision?"

Whiffles gasped so hard his bowtie spun.

"You don't know?"

"No."

"You poor, sweet pudding child. Realmvision is only the most glittering, emotionally turbulent, destiny-defining musical chaos event in all Ten Realms!"

"That told me nothing."

"It's like Eurovision... but with dragons, unresolved trauma, and interpretive dance intermissions."

"Still nothing."

Whiffles dropped into a crouch and whispered:

"Realmvision decides what happens next."

Aurelya blinked. "Like, in the story?"

"In every story."

"...that sounds like too much power for a talent show."

"Exactly." Whiffles beamed. "That's why it's fun!"

A mushroom behind them burst into applause.

Aurelya sat down, exhausted.

"I don't understand any of this," she sighed.

Whiffles patted her hand gently.

"No one does, Aurelya," he said. "The Realms are a dream. Dreams don't explain themselves. They ask you to play along."

She looked up at him.

"...What happens if I stop playing?"

Whiffles paused.

For once, he didn't answer.

Next, it's time to meet **Garry the Pigeon** everyone's favorite emotionally burnt-out sky gremlin has absolutely had it with the Realms and their narrative nonsense.

INTERMISSION

Plot Recap (Even Though Nothing Makes Sense)

So far in this not-quite-logical tale, we've encountered:

- Aurelya, who may or may not be glowing with destiny (or glitter, it's unclear).
- A lion in the clouds, but he's not Mufasa. He's probably more fabulous.
- A cactus who gives therapy advice, unprompted.
- Bubble croquet, which is now a thing.
- Realmvision, the most chaotic talent show since someone gave Loki a microphone.
- Whiffles, whose main hobbies include dramatic gasping and handing out metaphorical maps that might be cursed.
- A penguin on rollerblades yelling "FORESHADOWING!", which feels important. But we're not sure why.

We have absolutely no idea where this is going, but that's kind of the point.

There's magic, musicals, and a suspicious lack of
useful directions.

So grab a snack. Hug a succulent. And remember:

"Dream logic doesn't ask you to follow
it dares you to dance."

Now back to your regularly scheduled chaos.

Chapter 7: Garry the Pigeon is Done with This

Aurelya barely had time to process Whiffles' sudden silence before something thunked into her forehead.

"OW!"

It was a scroll.

Tied in blue string.

Slightly singed.

And it smelled like existential dread and popcorn.

She picked it up. The label read:

URGENT DELIVERY: FOR THE ONE WHO WON'T STOP ASKING QUESTIONS

A beat later, there was a flurry of feathers, a sharp squawk, and then... him.

Garry.
The pigeon.
The legend.

The unpaid, emotionally uninvested, no-nonsense courier of the Realms.

He landed on a signpost that immediately collapsed under the weight of his judgment.

Aurelya stared.

"...You're Garry?"

He adjusted his tiny mailbag and gave her a dead-eyed look.

"Yeah. What gave it away? The wings? The crippling disillusionment?"

"I've... heard about you."

"I hope it was from someone with high cholesterol. That's my target audience."

"What?"

"Never mind."

He rustled in his bag, pulled out another scroll, looked at it, rolled his eyes, and ate it.

"Was that important?" Aurelya asked.

"Not anymore."

She opened the scroll he'd delivered. It said:

You are dangerously close to the plot. Turn back. Or sing.

She looked up.

"I don't want to sing."

"Then you better turn back," Garry said, flapping to a boulder and pacing like a feathery war general. "You think you're in charge of this journey? Think again, Jam Girl."

"I have a name."

"Yeah? So, did I. Once."

"...What happened?"

"I saw the script."
He stared at her meaningfully.

"Page 83. I deliver a monologue that solves

everything. You know what happened to Page 83?"

She shook her head.

He hissed, "It was edited out."

"By who?"

Garry twitched. "The Author."

Aurelya paused.

"I thought the Author was… gone."

Garry shrugged. "They're always gone. Until they're not."

"…Do you always talk like this?"

"No. Sometimes I scream into jars."

Whiffles reappeared, bouncing on a pogo stick shaped like a fork.
"Oh no," he whispered. "Garry's reached meta-awareness."

Garry squawked. "Don't 'meta' me, Fork Hopper."

"I brought snacks!" Whiffles chirped, offering a basket of philosophical pears.

Garry knocked it off the stump. "We are not snackable feelings! We are unpaid cast members in an unlicensed dream!"

He flew up, hovered in front of Aurelya, and dropped a glitter-stained document into her hands.

It read:

REALMVISION PERFORMER CONTRACT
Terms: One performance, eternal consequences, zero refunds.

Aurelya gulped.

"Do I... have to sign this?"

Garry shrugged. "You already did. In Chapter One. While unconscious. It was in the pudding."

She stared.

He gave one last dead-eyed blink.

Then flew off muttering, "I was supposed to be a lawyer…"

Next, It's time for fish-flinging melodrama, icy interpretive tragedy, and penguins with *very* strong opinions about soliloquy pacing.

Welcome to the greatest theatrical disaster in the Ten Realms.

DONE WITH THIS

Chapter 8: The Shakespearean Penguins Present a Tragedy

The theatre was made of snow cones.

That was the first thing Aurelya noticed.

The second thing was the absolute silence.

Not the comforting kind the judgy kind.

Rows of penguins in Elizabethan collars sat in the audience, flippers folded, glaring like drama teachers waiting for someone to miss their cue.

Aurelya stood backstage, clutching a scroll that might have been a script, or possibly a deli order from three universes ago.

Next to her, Whiffles was powdering his nose with jellybeans.

"This is fine," he whispered. "This is totally fine."

"I'm not an actor," Aurelya hissed.

"You're in a dream. Everyone's an actor."

"I don't even know what this is."

"It's The Feathered Masque of Sorrows," said a penguin dramatically, emerging from a cloud of theatrical fog. "A tale of forks, fate, and poorly timed metaphor."

He handed her a costume: a giant spoon.

"I'm playing a salad fork," she said flatly.

"You are the Salad Fork of Destiny," the penguin corrected. "Your monologue is after the cheese collapse."

"...The what?"

But the stage was already rotating.

A voice boomed: ACT ONE: THE MELTING OF INTENTIONS.

Lights flashed. Fog poured. Dramatic violins screamed. A single sardine fell from above and hit the floor with a splat.
The crowd gasped.

Aurelya was pushed on stage.

"Do something," hissed a penguin in the wings.

So she stepped forward and cleared her throat.

"I... am... a fork."

Silence.

Then a lone penguin in the third row began to sob.

Aurelya blinked. "I pierce... the salad of existence. But I am not whole. I have... prongs. And doubts."

The sobbing intensified.

A penguin fainted.

Behind her, the set collapsed into an avalanche of cheese props.

"ACT TWO!" cried the narrator. "THE RISE OF THE GRATER."

Gerald (still wearing armour) waddled on stage holding a cheese grater and a daisy.

He gave her a look that said, just go with it.

She lifted her arms. "Oh, mighty Grater! Shred me not into insignificance!"

More sobbing. A sardine was thrown in tribute.

Whiffles wandered on dressed as a tragic leek.

"I was once broth," he wailed. "Now I am just seasoning."

ACT THREE: THE FORKING

Lights dimmed.

Aurelya stood alone, cheese dust in her hair, spoon costume askew.

"I was born a salad fork," she whispered. "But I dreamed of soup."

A hush fell over the audience.

One penguin screamed, "BRAVO!"

Another threw a rose made of frozen peas.

The curtain fell.

The snow cone stage melted.

And somewhere far away, a prophecy sneezed.

Backstage, Sir Sparkles sparkled.

"Darling," he said, pressing a glitter-stamped program into her hand. "That was the most delicious tragedy I've seen since the Flamingly Incident of '97."

"What just happened?" Aurelya asked, dazed.

"Emotional foreshadowing," Whiffles beamed. "You're a hit!"

"I improvised everything."

"Exactly. You were real."

"...And the cheese?"

"The cheese is always metaphorical."

Aurelya sighed.

The stage lights blinked out.

And a familiar scroll fluttered into her hand, this one

smelling faintly of regret and frosting.

REALMVISION REHEARSALS: FINAL CALL

Sir Sparkles clapped his hands twice.

"Places, everyone! It's time for the dress rehearsal!"

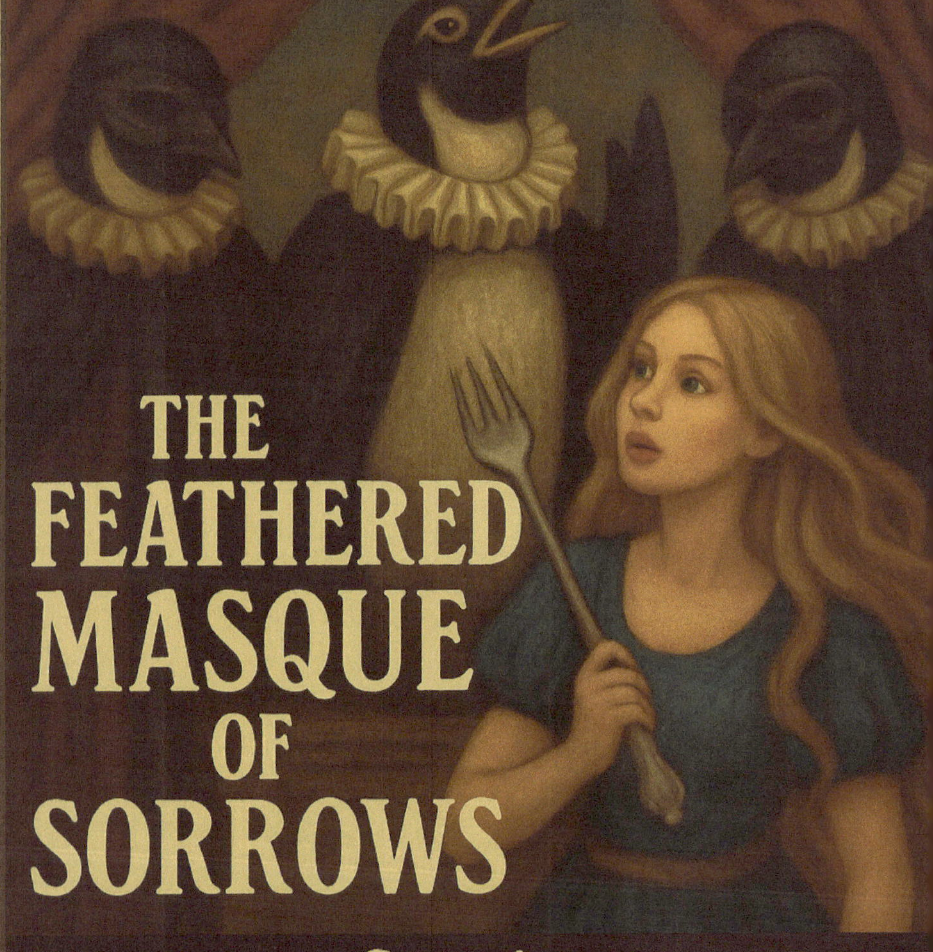

PLAYBILL
THE
FEATHERED
MASQUE
OF
SORROWS
Starring
Salad Fork of Destiny

Chapter 9: The Realmvision Rehearsals (Go Terribly Wrong)

The stage was alive.

Not metaphorically.

Literally.

It growled when people stepped on it, stretched like bread dough between performances, and once tried to eat Gerald's kazoo. Gerald didn't take it personally.

Aurelya stood side-stage, draped in a cape made from yesterday's newspaper headlines and future regrets. Her shoes were musical. Not just music-themed they actually sang every time she took a step.

"Step lightly," warned Whiffles, who was now in a full glitter unitard and wielding a clipboard that occasionally bit him.

"I don't know my song," Aurelya whispered.

"Perfect," said Sir Sparkles, descending from the ceiling in a gondola made of moonlight and tax forms. "Improvisation is the soul of chaos."

"I didn't sign up for this."

"You did," Sparkles said gently. "In pudding. Don't you read the terms and desserts?"

The lights dimmed.

Fog rolled in like someone spilled their feelings.

Sir Sparkles raised his sparkle-sceptre. "Begin rehearsal sequence!"

CONTESTANT ONE:
A sentient harmonica named Lou.
Song: "I Can't Breathe, I'm a Wind Instrument"
Result: Got stage fright and exploded.

CONTESTANT TWO:
A banshee on stilts.
Song: "Wail Me Maybe"
Result: Top notes shattered six teacups and part of the fourth wall.

CONTESTANT THREE:
Aurelya.
Song: "???????"

The music started.

Or didn't.

It sounded like a piano melting.

Aurelya froze.

Then Steve the Flamingo screamed, "DANCE OR DIE."

She danced.

Badly.

She spun. She tripped. Her shoes sang an off-key opera about regrets. Her cape caught fire (emotionally, not literally). She shouted the first words that came to her mind:

"I DON'T KNOW WHO I AM
BUT I'M WEARING A CAPE
AND THIS STAGE IS A NIGHTMARE
AND I'M FULL OF SHAPELESS HOPE"

The audience gasped.
A whale sobbed in the balcony.

Sir Sparkles wept glitter.

Aurelya finished with a flourish that was 40% panic

and 60% flailing.

Silence.

Then a single otter in the front row stood.

"Art," he whispered.

And fainted.

The stage hiccupped.

The scoreboard appeared it blinked wildly, scrambled its numbers, then displayed:

SCORE: ∞ EMOTIONAL DAMAGE / 1 DESTINY POINT

Sir Sparkles clapped. "Brilliantly broken! We must now… take a five-minute sob break."

Whiffles handed Aurelya a tissue shaped like a sock. "Am I done?" she asked.

"Oh no," Sparkles said, sipping tears from a crystal goblet. "You're not done."

He stepped closer.

"You've just qualified… for the Final Realmvision Showdown."

"…What?"

"You're going head-to-head with the reigning champion."

"Who is it?"

The lights dimmed again.

A hush fell over the stars.

And from the mist, a voice echoed:

"Did someone say… showdown?"

A figure stepped into the light.

Sequins. Shoulder pads. Fireworks.
It was…

Loki.

Next, where sequins meet fate, Loki absolutely *steals the stage*, and the Realms teeter on the edge of glittery collapse. Ready your heart. And your jazz hands.

REALMVISION

The Most Glittering, Gobsmacking, Chaotic Musical Destiny-thon in the Realms

MEET THE PERFORMERS!

THE KAZOO OF CONCUSSION

It is sentlent. Holds grodges, flat notes, and questionable flams,

NAGGIN' PUTRESCA THE BANSHEE

Anger management session just offstage. Do. Not. Ask.

DORLIA THE GNARLED MAGE

Are you in the audience? Or is she hallucinating again?

SIR SPARKLES

Fabulously renowned drag lion host. Objects keep catching on fire.

RULES: 1. HEARTBREAKING BALLADS ON LY. NO LIARS. NO ENCORES. 2. CHAOS IS MANDATORY

GLIT. GLAM. EMOTIONAL DAMAGE!

Chapter 10: The Realmvision Final

The stadium trembled.

Not with applause.

But with something deeper.
Like the dream itself was starting to realize it wasn't real.

Aurelya stood center stage, beneath a sky that had too many moons and a spotlight that flickered like it was running out of magic. Her cape whispered. Her shoes hummed nervously. Steve the Flamingo trembled in her arms.

And across from her… stood Loki.

He was flawless, of course.

Draped in sequins, shadows, and drama, grinning like a boy who just rewrote your diary and left helpful footnotes in glitter pen.

"Welcome to the end," he said.

"Of the show?" Aurelya asked.

He tilted his head.

"Sure. Let's call it that."

The Realmvision host otters marched out in sparkling formation. One tripped on a philosophical pretzel and was replaced by a duck.

Sir Sparkles floated overhead, teary-eyed and overly dramatic.

"Contestants!" he cried. "This is your final duet. Sing now… or vanish into narrative mist!"

Aurelya clutched the microphone.
It pulsed like a heartbeat.
A voice inside her whispered: "You're not supposed to be here."

ROUND ONE: THE DUET

Loki sang first.
A low, haunting melody called "I Never Meant to Break the Realms (But I Did It Anyway)"
The stars bent with every note.

Then Aurelya sang back a song that she didn't know until it was already leaving her mouth:

"I've seen this boy before
In places I've never been
He haunts the shape of silence
And smiles like a sin."

Her words shimmered. Then… cracked.
The spotlight shook. The stage let out a confused growl.
Audience members turned to fog.

ROUND TWO: SOMETHING WRONG

They danced. Sort of.

Loki moonwalked into a memory. Aurelya stumbled into a future.

Steve the Flamingo combusted into glitter.

The scoreboard blinked, trying to tally emotions it didn't understand.

SCORE: 1 Identity Crisis, 2 Plot Holes, 1 Tree

Aurelya fell to her knees.

The music stuttered.

Her voice echoed back too slowly, like the dream couldn't keep up.

Loki walked toward her, gently.

"You know what this is, don't you?" he asked.

Her lip trembled. "A dream?"

He smiled. Softer this time.

"Not just a dream. A goodbye."

FINAL NOTE

The lights shattered like stained glass.

Aurelya rose.

The stage fell away beneath her feet.

But still… she sang.

"If this is just a prelude
Then let the notes all bend
I'll wake before the story starts
And find you… at the end."

Loki whispered something she didn't hear.

The stadium vanished.

The song dissolved into starlight.

The last thing she saw was a tree.

Roots reaching through the dream like memory.

Chapter 11: The Snap Back to Reality

Everything was… floating.

Not her. Not exactly.
More like the world was loosening around her edges.

The sky blinked.
The stars rewound.

The stage was gone.

The Realmvision screams, the lights, the music all
faded into static like a television losing signal.

Aurelya reached for something. Anything.
But her hands passed through fog that remembered
being glitter.

Then she heard it:

"Wake up, petal."

A voice. Familiar and thorny.

The Talking Cactus.

He stood beside her on nothing at all, sipping from a
teacup made of sighs.

"You gave a lovely performance," he said.

"I... did I win?"

"No one wins," he replied. "It's not that kind of story."

She looked around. The space cracked. Tiny fissures
in the dream.
One corner folded like paper. Another leaked
starlight. Her cape unraveled into moths.

"Was any of it real?"

The cactus shrugged. "Does it matter?"

"Yes!"

"Then... yes. As long as you remember it."

Aurelya clutched her chest. "I do remember. The
Feast. The croquet. Whiffles. The show. Loki..."

The cactus sipped again. "Ah yes. The boy with too
many names."
"Will I see him again?"

"Oh, definitely. But you'll think it's the first time."

"Why?"

"Because you're waking up now."

She opened her mouth

And fell.

The fall wasn't fast.
It was slow. Gentle. Like the world was returning her
to herself with apology and affection.

Time bent.

Dreams unzipped.

Her pudding hat dissolved into melody. Steve the
Flamingo saluted and vanished. Sir Sparkles winked
as he faded.

Aurelya fell upward.

A breeze whispered:
"Let go, little story. The Realms are waiting."

She landed in light.

Soft moss. Cool air. The sound of a distant breeze rustling through very real trees.

Her dress was simple. Her hands were clean. No glitter. No music. No spotlight.

Just... stillness.

Just...

Chapter 12: The Boy Beneath the Tree

The grass was real.

She could feel it.

Cool. Damp. Rooted.

Aurelya opened her eyes.

No glitter. No flamingos. No singing shoes. Just the slow, steady light of early morning, soft and golden, like a secret being told for the first time.

Above her, the Tree of Life stretched into the sky.
Its branches curled like a crown.
Its bark shimmered faintly not with magic, but with memory.

She sat up.

Her body felt lighter. Not just in weight, but in pressure, like she'd been carrying something for so long she'd forgotten it wasn't part of her. Now, it was gone.

She looked down.

Her palms were empty.

But something in her chest…

…buzzed. Softly. Like the memory of music.

"You're awake," said a voice.

She turned.

He was leaning against the tree.

A boy, maybe a little older than her. Maybe a little younger than time. His coat was too dramatic for morning. His hair curled like mischief. And his smile… that smile…

"Hello," he said. "I'm Loki."

Aurelya didn't move.

Didn't speak.

Because something ached. Not in pain, in recognition. Like meeting someone again whom you hadn't realised you missed.

He raised an eyebrow. "You, okay?"

She nodded. Slowly.

"I had… a dream."

"Did it make sense?"

"Not even slightly."

"Good," he said, grinning. "The good ones never do."

He held out a hand.

She hesitated not out of fear, but out of knowing that everything, everything, was about to change.

Then she took it.

The Tree shimmered.

Somewhere far away, a cactus sipped his tea and said, "Here we go."

The Realms stirred.

The story began.

Whiffles Sends in a Little Squelch

A Realmsverse Intermission Tale

Aurelya had been minding her own business, mostly. She only meant to sniff the "Confidence Pudding," not inhale it.

But here she was wedged into the broom closet of Stage 3B, slowly inflating like a motivational balloon filled with regret.

Her legs poked through the ceiling. Her elbows had taken out a costume rack. And every time she sneezed, confetti burst from her ears.

"Whiffles?" she croaked.

"OH GOOD, YOU'RE AWAKE!" shouted Whiffles from somewhere outside. "Listen, Glorbella, we've got a bit of a tight schedule. Realmvision semifinals start in five minutes, and you've collapsed the glitter cannon booth."

"My name's not"

"No time for identity!" Whiffles yelled, shoving a scroll under the door with instructions written entirely in rhyming riddles and custard stains. "I've sent in Squelch. He'll fix it."

There was a pause. Then, the sound of wet slapping.

Slap. Slap. Squidge.

Aurelya blinked just as a tiny mushroom-shaped creature squelched under the door and peered up at her with heroic determination and absolutely no eyebrows.

"SQUELCH REPORTING FOR DUTY!" it shouted proudly. "PREPARED TO CLIMB, MA'AM."

"Climb what?"

"You, mostly."

Squelch strapped on suction cups made of jellybeans and began scaling her left leg. "I've trained for this moment in the Swamp of Inconvenient Staircases."

"Please tell me there's a shrinking potion or a magic reset button"

"Nope. Just Squelch."

Meanwhile, Whiffles had gathered a crowd of Realmvision interns outside who were throwing emotional pebbles at the door. (They screamed things like "YOU'RE DOING YOUR BEST!" and "YOUR FAILURE IS VALID!")

The pebbles turned into tiny affirmation cakes. One rolled toward Aurelya's swollen foot. She ate it.

Poof.

She shrank too fast, bounced off the mop bucket, and landed directly in a tutu hanging from the top hook of the closet.

Squelch landed in a glitter trap but saluted anyway.

Whiffles peeked in.

"Well done, Glorbella! Quick, get her a clipboard. She's hosting the backup intro for the Realmvision intermission skit about emotionally intelligent spoons."

Aurelya stared blankly.

"I'm never sniffing pudding again."

Squelch winked.

"That's what they all say."

[End of Bonus Chapter]

A
A

K
K

About the Author

Holly Symons is the whimsical architect behind the Realmsverse, a world where celestial crowns, sarcastic squirrels, and misplaced prophecies collide. With a lifelong love of myth, magic, and mischief, Holly weaves heartfelt fantasy with a generous dash of comedy.

Aurelya in Wonderrealm is a playful prequel to her beloved Realm Shatter Saga, taking readers on a dreamlike romp through absurd logic and deep emotion. Whether she's wrangling enchanted lions or rewriting reality with a flaming quill, Holly's storytelling always champions courage, chaos, and the weirdly wonderful.

When not crafting Realmsverse tales, she enjoys long daydreams, Nordic folklore, and pretending talking animals are giving her life advice. She writes from Australia, surrounded by books, tea, and characters who refuse to stay on the page.

www.ingramcontent.com/pod-product-compliance
Lightning Source LLC
Chambersburg PA
CBHW042035180726
48295CB00006B/105